Luke the Unexpected

USA Today Bestselling Author

Dani Haviland

Dedicated to those in my life, both those who live near and those who engage with me in cyberspace, to those who read my works, support my efforts, tolerate my obsession with writing: a huge hug and sincere thank you.

A special shout out to Mary Kelley and Gayle Hartman-Weatherford for helping me select vehicles for my story. I love classic/vintage cars and motorcycles, so they're essential in my characters' lives, too.

~NOTE~ This novella is a stand-alone story but occurs just after the story of (and includes) Benji, the young man in *Pool Boy Wanted: No Experience Preferred.*

Rural North Carolina, Autumn 1997:

Brought together by their love of vintage motorcycles, Luke and Holly have more than just an out of tune Indian Chief to deal with. The spurned Tanya wants revenge and will stop at nothing to hurt Luke and all those he cares about.

1 Skin Deep

Autumn 1997

Smack!

"Where... What... Who was that?" Robbie called as he spun around, grasping his now throbbing nose.

The blubber-bellied teenager pulled the yellow-haired girl closer with his one free arm, looking for movement behind the piles of broken refrigerators and stoves and the wire baskets of scrap metal.

How could he have missed someone punching him in the snout? He had double-checked to make sure the old junkyard was deserted before he sliced through the plastic wire-tie that secured the gap in the chain link fence. After all, he didn't want anyone witnessing the attitude adjustment he was going to give the smart-mouthed, prick-teasing blonde. No one got away with calling him Tubby, even if—no, especially if—it was a girl.

He'd never pummeled a girl before. Well, except for his

last foster mother, but he was just defending himself. Besides, that didn't count since no one pressed charges and she was jailed for worse stuff a month later. He was 18 now, a lone wolf, emancipated from the system, and he'd handle problems and problem-makers his own way.

"I'm right here, bully," Luke whispered huskily at the side of Robbie's shaggy head.

Robbie turned to face the stranger. "How'd you get in here?" he asked, wiping his bloody nose on the shoulder of his mis-buttoned plaid shirt. "And why did you hit me? I didn't do anything to you!"

The unexpected hero in threadbare jeans and a white tee shirt turned away, ignoring the oversized teenager with the bad attitude and offered the sobbing girl his hand. "Are you all right?" he asked.

"Who are you?" Tanya replied, wide-eyed at seeing anyone else on this deserted property. She had made sure she and Tubby would be alone. And, although she was new in this small town, she would have remembered seeing a man this good-looking and broad-shouldered— here or anywhere!

"Hey!" Robbie stepped over and wedged himself in

between the blonde damsel in distress and her dark-haired knight.

Luke's eyes narrowed as he assessed the cad, noted his unsteady stance, then gave him a well-placed hip bump, knocking him to the ground.

"That's twice you've knocked me for a loop," Robbie said. "You're a marked man now, Asshole!"

"Marked? Nope." Luke rolled up the short sleeves on his cotton tee shirt to the top of his shoulders, flexing his muscles slightly to antagonize the chunky man-child even more. "Not marked. No tats on me anywhere. At least, that are visible," he added with a wink to the stunned femme. "And you got my name wrong, too. It's Luke. It's a simple mono-syllabic moniker. It should be easy for you to remember."

"You won't be around long enough for…"

Luke had turned his attention back to the young, stunned woman, once again deliberately ignoring the boor.

All bullies were alike. They talked big, yelled loud, pushed and shoved those smaller than themselves, and somehow—without any specialized schooling—managed to excel in the science of intimidation.

"Hey, I'm talking to you..." Robbie tried again to get the newcomer's attention, this time gripping Luke's shoulder from behind.

Luke grabbed the grimy paw, squeezed fingers together until he heard a whimper, then spun away, twisting the sweaty arm up and behind the youth until he looked as if he had a duck wing, not an arm.

"Hmm. I'll bet this is your favorite position. At least, for your victims. I'd call you by your given name, but I really don't care enough about you to ask for it. And, since I believe you were planning on visiting some distant relative in a neighboring town — or better yet, a distant state — I'll not bother. Now, the lady and I were just getting acquainted, so skedaddle and take your broken knife with you."

Luke held out the knife he had surreptitiously filched during the arm-twisting do-si-do.

"But it's not broke," Robbie said, reaching for it.

"Well, I'll be." Luke flicked opened the switchblade, dropped it to the ground, then used his boot to nudge it on top of a half-buried stone. He stomped down with his size 13 Wellington, separating the six-inch blade from its plastic faux-bone hilt.

"Oh, and don't even think about complaining to the cops or anyone else. That type of 'shaving razor' is illegal. I doubt you'd want to admit to any of your so-called friends that the new guy in town bested you, either."

"But...but..."

"No, dude, it's bye, bye. Can you repeat after me? Bye." Luke paused and sucked in his lips in exaggeration, then exhaled as he enunciated, "Bye," and walked away, the young blonde clinging to his arm.

"You'll get yours," Robbie fumed, his face scarlet, the urge for revenge overwhelming his common sense. He pulled back to kick the softball-sized stone the muscular jerk had used to destroy his favorite blade, then decided that would probably break his foot. Instead, he field-goal kicked a pile of gravel toward the disappearing couple with the inside of his red and white Air Jordan cross trainer. The earthen projectiles dissipated in the afternoon breeze, not even the dust making it to his new number one enemy, Luke

He walked back to the hole in the fence, the secret entrance he had found to 'Tanya's Haven,' then turned back and called, "Asshole."

Luke shook his head. They were all alike. Dense,

stubborn, foolish. "You got it wrong again. It's Luke. Just Luke." He shook his head and thought, 'What a shame. With a different attitude, we could have been friends.'

"Come on," the blonde said, pulling Luke's arm to follow her.

Luke glanced over his shoulder. Maybe he had been a little rough on the bloated cream puff, but he had learned long ago to take down the biggest, baddest jerk in the yard— or town, or school—so he wouldn't have to worry about watching his back. Or not getting the girl.

She parted an overhanging honeysuckle vine, disclosing a well-trodden path. "This is where he dragged me in."

Warning sirens went off in Luke's head. 'The kid just left the way they came in. Why the lie?'

"I said, have you been in town long?" she repeated, her blush showing through her freckles. "I've only been here two months, but I'm sure I'd remember seeing you…"

"Sorry. I was just making sure we were safe. No, I just got here. I saw him pulling you along. I wasn't sure if you were following of your own volition or not."

Luke could see by her blank stare that she didn't understand him. "I mean, I wasn't sure if you wanted to go with him or not. Look, you're a very pretty girl and he's not, well... Let's just say, he wouldn't be a candidate for America's hottest bachelor contest, much less a winner."

Her coy smile broadened as she lifted her hand to him. "Hi, I'm Tanya, by the way," she cooed, then bit her bottom lip suggestively. Then, rather than accept the hand he offered in return as a handshake, she walked into him—entrenching herself in his personal space—then reached up and caressed his face. She slid her hands over his ears and cupped them, bringing his face down to hers.

"Um," he stalled as he gently pulled her hands away. "I thought we were going back to town."

Tanya would not be deterred. Fresh meat. She was ready for another ribbon in her bouquet of beaus. Blue would be the right color for him. Light blue for Luke; like his tight-fitting jeans. He didn't look to have much money, but if he was a good lay, she'd let him have the first date for free. Then he could join her select group of thieves. Fagin had nothing on her. She was so much more than that leader of Oliver Twist, the Artful Dodger, and that pathetic group of pickpockets from the story they made her read in high school.

Luke turned away from her, nearly choking on the taste of bile rising. Whether her glare of greed was for his body or what she could get from him didn't matter. Maybe the young man had been the victim earlier, and he had shoved away the wrong one.

Tanya could tell she was losing him. It was time for a different tactic. She pressed close to him and slithered around to press herself against the bulge behind his Levi buttons. She snorted as she realized it was not hard as it had appeared a moment ago. She rubbed against him suggestively, hoping to bring it back to life. Now he was a challenge. She just had to have him back as an adoring fan. She locked her hands around the back of his neck, then wrapped one leg around his body to bring him even closer to her warm spot that was getting moister by the second.

Luke settled his hands gently over hers. "Oh, darlin'" he cooed, then turned away from her, disengaging from her unwelcome boa constrictor hold.

Tanya took a step back and stood tall, her hands now fisted on her low-rider short shorts. "What? You play for the other team?" She blatantly stared down at his crotch and shook her head in disbelief. That could be the only answer to his refusal of her 'you can't say no to this' come on. Shoot, she was even wearing her best push up bra! Then she remembered Shawn.

"You know, I'd sure like to see that bean pole of yours when it's happy. I have a friend, Shawn. He plays both sides. I'm sure we can have a *ball* together. A great big, fu..."

Luke clamped a hand over her mouth, putting his other behind her head to make sure she didn't disengage from his physical censoring.

"Watch your words, woman! I thought there was a lady present, but I guess I was mistaken. Still, some words are better left unsaid. Now, I assume you're familiar with this, this..."

Luke looked around. Now that they were beyond the scrap metal yard, he saw it. The shanty patio she had led him to was an impromptu storage site. Stacks of boxes piled under the lean-to addition–new boxes marked VCRs, TVs, and microwaves—made it look like a Costco showroom without the pallet racking. "I suppose this is *your* business..."

Luke didn't finish his sentence, but she did after she wiggled out of his hold. "You're damned right this is my business! And it's none of yours! You'd better not tell anyone about it, either. Not that you'd get anywhere letting the cat out of the bag. Folks wouldn't believe that sweet little Tanya would do anything illegal. And the cops… Well, they're on the take. Some with a few extra bucks here and there, some get a sweet little f…"

Luke popped the bottom of her chin with the side of his index finger, slamming her mouth shut and stifling that debasing and disgusting word before it escaped again.

"You made me bite my lip, you…you Asshole!"

"As I told your little friend earlier, my name is Luke."

"Not now, it's not. It's Mud."

Luke strode away from the swearword-slinging blonde, shaking his head in self-admonishment. Should he throw a snappy comeback at her? *'I may be mud, but adobe buildings and villages were made of that wet, earthy substance, and they've survived the ravages of time and storms for centuries. Piles of shit like you don't last a season. They're only good as food for dung beetles and slugs,'* went through his mind, but he'd stick with his gut feeling. Keep away from her. She wasn't worthy of any more of his time or wit.

How could he have been so wrong about that situation?

10

Yes. Of course. Once again, he had let the coy giggles and provocative clothing of a good-looking woman get in the way of his common sense.

He was tempted to turn back to at least see the expression on her face. Was she determined to take him down with the little gang she had just put together in the last two months? Would the cops do her bidding and make life miserable for him? He chuckled. They couldn't stop him for fictitious traffic violations because he didn't own a car, much less a motorcycle, his preferred mode of transportation.

Nah. If she had been honest and really did have cops on the take...

And there it was. Nothing about her was honest, not even the color of her dark-rooted hair. He needn't fear the law. A chill ran up his back and it wasn't just sweat evaporating. He would have to watch out for her — all the time —and her starry-eyed, lust-driven minions.

"Beauty is only skin deep, but ugly goes clear to the bone," he reminded himself aloud, hoping that maybe this time, he'd finally learn. At least today, no one was harmed— not really—and no money was stolen.

2 Homecoming

The gaudy yellow and blue sign loomed over the shop: Matt's Repair Shop: If we can't fix it, _____

Luke chuckled as he recalled some of the answers Matthew had given prospective customers about the underlined blank space at the end of the banner. The first time he asked his uncle, he wouldn't give him a direct answer. He thought he was being rude, but now he understood what it was all about. "Just watch and learn, young man. I can tell if I want a person as a customer or not by the way he handles that sign."

And, sure enough, that open-ended banner was the culling process for a whole lot of ornery people. "What? Don't trust your own work? Looking for an excuse before you even check my car to see what the problem is? Couldn't afford to buy a few more words for the rest of your sign?"

As Luke stared up at the new polycarbonate version of the old floppy banner, a spritely gray-haired man came out to greet him. He stood shoulder-to-shoulder with him and stared up. "It's not the same sign, but I decided to use the same format." He turned to Luke, bumped upper arms with him, grinned and said, "Hey, there, Luke! How's it going?"

Luke turned and gave his uncle a hearty handshake that quickly turned into a big bear hug. Then they both looked back at the sign and wondered what to say or do next.

"You see, Luke," Matt said, and took a deep breath, knowing words would pop out on their own when it came to talking with his long overdue nephew, "Some things never change. People have to trust you and you need to have a bit of confidence in them, too. What if a man came in and said, 'I just need an oil change,' and I discover that he had run the engine out of oil two years ago and had just refilled it before he came in here; it was now ready to throw a rod? Don't you think he'd tell the whole town what a rip off I was, how I couldn't even do a little oil change without trashing his motor? Nah, a signed work order is only so good. I can read a bit about a potential client in the intake process, when he's telling me about the problem with his car or tractor or what not. But that first meeting, when they see that sign..." Matt shook his head and grinned. "Yup, I've given dozens, maybe hundreds of answers to 'what does that mean' over the years. But just about every one was tailored to the man or woman asking it."

Luke chuckled in recall. "Remember when Joey Fetko came in with that dead bird wrapped in a dish towel and wanted you to fix it?"

"Well, if you remember, I took care of him, but I didn't make his mother too happy. I told him I couldn't fix it—it was already dead—but I could offer him an upgrade. I gave him one of the kittens old Fluffy had kicked out six weeks before." Matt scratched his head. "Come to think about it, Joey was in here last month. He said he still had that cat. And Fluffy. His mother said she'd take the mama cat, too. Had her fixed right away, so no more kitties. I'll bet that was at least ten years ago…"

Luke nodded in agreement. He'd been saying he'd come back to help his uncle for two years, at least, but the gentle old guy never complained or harped.

"Do you still need a hand, Unc?" he asked sheepishly.

Matthew chortled. "I always have enough work for at least one more mechanic than I have in coveralls. Sure. Come on in and give us a hand. I want you to meet some of the others. I'll bet your talent didn't disappear overnight, or even in the last five years. Natural-born diagnosticians don't show up at your doorstep every day." Matthew slapped Luke on the back, "I didn't think you'd make it. I mean, it's been what, six months, since you were supposed to show up for the job?"

"You know me: Luke, the unexpected…"

"Yes, but you're usually unexpected as in showing up to save someone's bacon in the nick of time, not… Well, I'm just glad you made it."

Matthew held the door open for Luke, then paused, letting his nephew take in the vast changes he'd made in the last few years. "Oh, shoot. I just remembered. I have to run downtown to pick up a few parts. Go ahead and make yourself at home. I'll be back in a few minutes."

Luke walked into the outer showroom. "Did you miss me?" he announced.

He immediately felt stupid. Old Aunt Maude wasn't at the desk behind the parts counter as she had been for the last twenty years. The mountains of mixed colored papers— invoices and receipts to be paid or mailed out—were also missing. He looked around. She wasn't anywhere. What he saw instead scared him on two levels.

Organization. Two towers of filing trays, barren save a few sheets of paper, were on top of the only desk in the room. Uncle Matt thrived on chaos and Maude's bookkeeping skills, although effective to a degree, were as unconventional as throwing the Sunday newspaper in the air on a windy day and watching the bits and pieces slide downhill.

Then he saw the desk jockey: the most gorgeous blonde he had ever seen. Hair almost white, long and straight. And no dark roots. Flawless skin without a touch of makeup…

His stomach clenched. It was beginning to look as if Matthew no longer owned the shop. He'd never let anyone save Aunt Maude handle the books. Had something happened to him and he had lost the shop because he forgot to pay the mortgage? Again?

Luke took a deep breath and blew it out, shaking his head slightly as he looked at the beauty behind the big CRT monitor. Blondes and good looks: they were a dangerous combo. Or could be.

'Never judge a book by its cover,' he whispered softly, then approached the apparent receptionist. Or, by the looks of orderly paperwork, very capable office manager.

"Madam, I mean, Miss, is Maude in today?"

The young lady wearing the white 'Matt's Place' tee shirt smiled, nodded, and then reached under the desk and pushed the buzzer by her knee.

Luke sauntered away, not wanting to crowd her, and perused the latest hot rod posters on the wall above the display tires. He pointed to the souped up garbage truck. "It looks like Matthew got rid of the racy girly posters," he said, then turned back to see her reaction.

None. Not a snort of disgust or a twitter of a laugh at his reference to the scantily clad women showing off wrenches or hawking oil filters. Maybe she hadn't heard him, but his comment wasn't worth repeating. Looks like he'd dodged defending what could be construed as a sexist remark.

"I had Matt take them down to reflect what we do around here, not what some of these squirrelly guys want to have parked in their garages. We want to show them what is really possible to have," Maude said. "How are you doing, Luke? Long time, no see."

Luke embraced his aunt with a bit more zest than he thought he should, but his relief was great. She was still alive, even if she no longer was the woman behind the desk.

"I'm fine, but I was a bit scared when I didn't see you.

Are you okay? I mean, I heard you'd been under the weather..."

"Not under the weather. I'm fine. Clean bill of health. I just needed to step away from the stress for a while. Matt let me take a 'semi-retirement' to indulge myself in whatever I wanted. Yes, I had a minor heart issue three years ago, but Holly has the paperwork and billing under control, so I don't see why I should come back. I just dropped in to see if I could take your uncle out to lunch. I guess he went on a quick parts run. No worries. Now you can join us for a bite so we can catch up on what's been going on in your life."

Maude grasped him by the elbow and turned him around. "Luke, meet Holly, the best dam...darned bookkeeper in the whole state of North Carolina." She leaned into Luke's ear and whispered, "And the prettiest."

Luke nodded and said, "A pleasure to meet you, Holly. I sure admire the way you've cleaned up the place."

Holly smiled, then bowed her head in humility. A spark of recall lit her face, and she held up a short stack of two-part checks to Maude.

"Oh, it looks like it's time to empty the kitty," she said with a laugh. "I'm still a check signer, after all."

Holly then picked up a stack of stamped envelopes and pointed to the 'outgoing mail' tray and set them in it.

"Oh, and she already has the statements processed so we can fill up the bank account again. In and out. Sometimes I wonder if it's worth it."

Holly shook her finger at her in admonishment, then pointed to the newly remodeled lobby.

"You got that right, Holly. And I can craft and paint all day, am eating well, and we're still able to help put food on a few more tables in this area. Oh, and Luke, speaking of employees, I want you to meet Benji."

Luke looked up and saw a tall, broad-shouldered youth with the brightest red hair he'd ever seen walking towards him. The two reached out and shook hands.

Luke cleared his throat and nodded in silent greeting. This was the starting point of a new working relationship. Two men shaking hands for the first time. Would one squeeze the other's hand, looking to assert dominance? Nope. Benji's grip was firm enough to be confident, but gentle enough to let Luke know he wasn't trying to be the alpha. As Uncle Matt always said, 'you can't judge a book by its cover, but a man's handshake says volumes.'

Maude continued the introduction, "Matthew's cousin Alisha sent him in with a referral a few months back. I was expecting you to be here by then, so he helped fill the void while you, ahem, finished your business. Benji's a fast learner, too."

"And yer Aunt Maude is a great cook," Benji said, trying to deflect the compliment that had reddened his face. "Who would want to leave a set up like this? Good eats," Benji nodded to Maude, "a great teacher in Matthew," then turned to face away from Holly, "and the scenery…" Benji winked at Luke. He turned back towards the lady behind the desk and continued speaking to Luke. "These hills and streams: the finest trout fishing since I left Scotland."

Holly grinned at the men but remained silent. As always, she knew they were speaking about her. But, without a doubt, it wasn't in a negative manner. She might be deaf as a candle, but she could read people as well — no, better — than she could read lips.

Benji looked over at his employer's nephew. "Come on back and see what's in the works. With Matthew's reputation, there's always a wheeled, winged, or track-type vehicle lined up, waiting for repair."

"Or souping up," Maude added. "I'm sure glad Holly wrote up that new service work order with the disclaimer 'Any changes or modifications from factory specifications done per client request are at his/her own risk/peril/discretion and are not covered by any warranty, expressed or implied.'"

"Aye, and ye wouldn't believe the sorts of enhancements we've made. Did ye ken that next week is the first annual riding mower competition? Ye missed the garbage truck races last week."

Holly shook her head and rolled her eyes. 'Men,' she said loud and clear without a sound whispering past her lips.

3 Working For a Living

"Let me introduce you to the triplets," Benji said dramatically. His long arm pulled back the slatted vinyl curtains that separated the shop from the front office/parts counter. "Johnny, Cubby, and Husky, otherwise known as John Deere, Cub Cadet, and Husqvarna." The red, yellow, and green garden tractors parked in the bays sported oversized tires and shock absorbers, sponsor decals, extra chrome, and other ostentatious non-factory modifications.

"Yer uncle and I have souped these up for the First Annual Riding Lawn Mower Championship. Holly is a whiz at advertising, too. We even had one of the guys from that TV tool show come in and check them out. I think they're going to do an episode about it." Benji chuckled, then grunted like a big animal, "Huh, huh, huh! Pretty cool, aye?"

"Aye," Luke agreed. "And they're turbocharged, too? Oh, and what's this I hear about super-high horsepower garbage truck modifications? Was that Holly's idea, too?"

"Nah. She read about it in one of the trades. Having the

posters up was her idea. We don't sell any of that over-powered stuff, but once the guys come in, they go ahead and schedule brake jobs, tune ups, tire rotations, whatever."

"So, are you two an item? Do you have dibs on her?" Luke asked, his eyes avoiding Benji's.

"Dibs? Oh, ye mean do I have my heart set on her? No. And dinna think ye can play around with *her* heart. Holly is a wonderful lass. No, wait. No matter her age, she's a classy lady. I think of her as a sister, so dinna be toyin' with her heart…or anything else. Besides, I think yer uncle would castrate ye like a ruttin' billy goat if ye caused her pain or distress."

"So, what about the other ladies in town?" Luke asked, hoping to turn the conversation to Tanya, whether she was a potential risk to him or just a floozy.

"I have no idea. I've given up on women for a while. I, shall we say, had a verra bad experience with one a few months past. Besides, I think Holly likes having someone near her age not hitting on her. She says I'm the brother she never had."

"So, she does talk?" Luke asked.

Benji inhaled deeply, trying to compose an answer that

wasn't a lie, but also wouldn't betray her confidence. He held up both hands, stained black from changing the timing chain on the mayor's blue '67 Chevy Malibu, and fidgeted back and forth with them, wildly moving his fingers in front of his face. "I picked up a little sign language over the years. Then your Aunt Maude let me borrow her ASL for Beginners book. Most beginner series books use the phrase 'for dummies' in there somewhere, but ironically, not this one. I dinna ken if you ken it or not, so I'll tell you. Calling a Deaf person a dummy is verra derogatory. I've never seen Holly lose her cool over some idiot referring to her as that, but there's sure a lot of fire being held back at times. Oh, and make no mistake about it—she's an excellent lip reader. She told me once that people don't realize that their body language is just as important in a conversation as words. She'll pick up on that, too."

Luke nodded and blew out a big breath. He was attracted to her, but she seemed extremely complex.

"Don't let me scare ye away from her, Luke. She's a wonderful young lass, but one ye'd like to make yer wife, not just have as a summer fling."

Luke pointed his finger at Benji, using his own version of

sign language to say, 'You've got a good point there, buddy,' then changed the subject. "So, you've only been here a short time then?"

"I came here a few months back to bust tires, sweep floors, whatever it took to have a dry spot to sleep and a bite to eat. Turns out, Matthew was willing to teach me a trade. Or six. Yer uncle is a university of knowledge. One day, he's training me how to cut off old tracks and weld on new grousers, and the next day how to adjust the ailerons on a Super Cub. That's a mighty small but powerful plane, by the way."

"I'm familiar with PA-18s," Luke said, nodding that he understood. He didn't want to brag about his extensive training, but didn't want to be thought ignorant, either.

He walked away, looking up at the walls covered with belts and hoses, down the narrow aisles between parts bins, toolboxes, and shop carts. "Benji, this shop seems a lot smaller than I remember. Then again, I was only thirteen or so and pretty scrawny last time I was here. Uncle Matthew told me I had promise, and that if I ever wanted to be a mechanic, he'd train me. After my folks divorced, we kinda lost track of each other. But, still, I've managed to get my share of time under hoods, cowlings, and tracks."

"Aye, he split up the work areas. He has another shop across the backyard from this one. One bay is for planes and the other three for heavy equipment. So, have ye worked on those, too?"

"Like his business cards say, 'We fix anything with wheels, wings, or tracks.' I sent him a very brief resume a few months ago, letting him know what I'd been up to. I was supposed to be here sooner, but, um, life sort of got in the way."

"It happens. If ye want to hear the Lord laugh, tell Him yer plans." Benji chuckled at his own joke, then pointed to the shelves. "I heard yer Aunt Maude say she was going to take ye and yer uncle out to lunch. When ye get back, head on over to the big shop. Lewis, the lead mechanic, will line you up with a work order. It's Friday. We'll wind down around 4:00, wash up, go home for a bit, and then head to Aunt Maude's for popcorn and maybe a few hands of cards or a movie. She and Matthew have a huge collection of VHS tapes. Ye see, Maude hates commercials. She doesn't care fer rewinding the tapes, either, so if yer enjoyin' the shows with her, ye get to do the rewindin' when it's done. She has this little Corvette-looking plastic gizmo that's actually a tape rewinder she'll let ye use. It also saves time between movies. If we start early enough and don't have any Saturday projects, we might get a double feature."

Matt's voice rang out, "You two look like a couple of young hounds, sniffing each other's butts, figuring out who's the top dog." He poked his head between the floppy vinyl panels and added, "See, I told you I'd be back soon."

"Matt, that's horrible," Aunt Maude said, and punched Uncle Matt's shoulder as he held the panels back for her. "Come on, Luke. It's never a good idea to keep a woman waiting, especially when she's hungry. And didn't you say you were taking all of us out to lunch? I'm sure that Benji's hungry, too…"

"Ye ken I'm always ready for a bite, but I really want to get this done before the weekend gets here. How about jest bringing me back a piece of pie. Any kind. Ye ken me."

"Yes, dear," Maude said. "I'll see if they have a nice fluffy cream pie so you won't miss the a la mode part. I don't think cherry pie would taste too good after sitting in the box, the ice cream making the crust all soggy. Besides, we're just having lunch. We'll still have corn dogs and snacks at our place this evening. Take care, now, Benji."

Matthew guided his two lunch dates out the back door of the shop, waved good-bye to Benji, then asked, "Luke, when was the last time you had a big plate of barbecue and roasted corn on the cob?"

"Honestly, it was so long ago that I can't remember when."

"Then it's set," Maude declared. "We'll have a proper coming home dinner soon. I don't want to go half-way with it, so it may take me a day or two to get the menu set. Asides, I have to get that old stove fixed before I can make a proper batch of corn fritters."

"Don't worry about that, Maude. I told you, I have it under control."

Maude winked at Matthew and said, "I'm sure you do, dear. In the meantime, it's back to The Pink Cadillac for meals. We'll get you set up with the biggest, creamiest biscuits and gravy you ever sank your teeth into. Shoot, they're so good, I don't even fix them for us. We just go there and eat!"

4 The Pink Cadillac

Matt held the passenger door open for Maude as she slid into the front of the black and gold classic '57 Mercury Turnpike Cruiser, allowing Luke to get in the back seat by himself.

Luke looked up as they pulled into The Best Darned Diner. "Uncle Matt, I've always wanted to know, why in the heck is that pink Cadillac up there? I mean, it looks to be in perfect shape — save that broken-out wing window — but isn't that an over-the-top sign for a greasy spoon restaurant?"

"Well, Luke, there's a story behind that, for sure. Oh, and it isn't a greasy spoon. They still have the best half-pound burgers this side of the Mississippi. And like your Aunt Maude said, if you're jones-ing for biscuits and gravy, this is the place."

Matt pulled up and parked in the 'reserved' spot and shut down the engine. "Still hums like it's brand new."

He pulled open the glass front door with the big 'push' label on it. "Allow me," he said, and ushered Maude and Luke in first, then nodded to the waitress, letting her know he'd take his usual booth. Luke slid in next to Aunt Maude at the table in the back by the big bay window, then noticed the little brass plaque on the wall next to them. 'Reserved for Matthew and Maude when they're in the mood for great food.'

"But about that car, Luke," Matt said, eager to continue the story of the giant pink sedan parked on the pole. "You see, it used to be a-ridin' all over town car. Ol' Edna Worthington loved that Cadillac but didn't know how to drive. But her husband, Jim Bob, did. Well, every Saturday night she'd get all dolled up, just waiting for Jim Bob to come home from work and take her out to dinner and a movie. By the way, he was the top salesman at the Cadillac dealership and she was a stay at home wife. He had bought that Caddie fair and square — more or less, give or take a kickback or three on the tires and custom paint job — a few years earlier.

"Well, Edna waited and waited for Jim Bob to come home that one Saturday night, getting angrier and meaner as the hours went by. He finally come sauntering in about midnight, drunker than a bar-dwelling skunk. Said he didn't love her, never had, and that she had been third on his short list of women to wed. She was, however, first in the rich daddy department. And since her looks were passable and the food at the diner — meaning this place — was utterly scrump-dilli-uptious so he didn't care if she could cook or not, well, he decided he'd marry her."

Matthew chuckled when he saw Luke notice the plaque. "They had it put on there about a year ago, after I decided I'd make their take-out menu available at the parts and service counter." He cleared his throat and continued his local history lesson.

"'Too bad you never gave me a son,' he told her, 'but that's a good thing, too. You see, it looks like I'm getting one from another source. Betty Jean. You know, the cutie who was Princess of Pioneer Valley Creameries last year? Well, Betty Jean is going to give me a boy.'"

Matthew snorted and added, "Edna told me about it later. She said she had that cast iron skillet at the ready, twirling the handle back and forth twixt her fingers and thumb, just itching for a chance to bean that pot-bellied cheater, then she thought better of it.

"'You say she's with child?' she asked.

"'Yes, she is,' Jim Bob gloated.

"'You do know that she couldn't be more than 17 years

31

old. She was and is a classmate of Linda Sue Kellogg. As I recall, they're both supposed to graduate from high school next year.'

"Jim Bob narrowed his eyes, suspicious of what she was telling him, then gulped as he realized he had admitted not just adultery but having sexual relations with a minor.

"'Tongue-tied, are you?' Edna taunted, the skillet still held tight in her hand. "I'll tell you what. I'll give you a divorce so you can marry that child. You did know she was dirt poor, didn't you? I mean, I've always known you married me for my daddy's money, but I guess Betty Jean can be the one you married for love.'

"'But, but,' Jim Bob stammered, his hands flying up to the sides of his head to slick back his Brylcreem-saturated hair.

"'Oh, that's right,' Edna continued. 'You didn't say you loved her. You wanted her so she could give you a son. Well, lots of luck with that. She's one of eight girls — the middle child —and her mother told me she was up to eight granddaughters now. Not a male child born to her or her five sisters in generations.'

"'But, but…'

"'You'd better get that 'but-ter' fixed before you get yourself into more trouble. I'll go to the courthouse Monday, fill out all the papers with Travis Joe — he's my first cousin, you see, and owes me a favor. Not that he wouldn't do it anyway… He'll bring the paperwork to you at the dealership, get a few witnesses for the signatures, and then high-tail it back to the courthouse for the filing. I'm not sure how many days, but he'll let you know. As soon as it's final, you and little Miss Betty Jean can get hitched. But you better stay faithful to her or tie that little thing of yours in a knot.'

"At that point, Edna laughed out loud, held up her pinkie finger, and wiggled it, saying, 'I don't know how you could tie something that short in a knot, but,' then laughed again.

"That Monday afternoon, there was such a to-do when it came time for the signing that they're still talking about it at the dealership.

"'I'm not giving her that pink Cadillac! She can't even drive! She can have the house, the furniture, everything else, but not the Caddie!'

"'Well, Edna was there, too. She'd snuck in right after her cousin gave Jim Bob the papers, expecting the big fuss and wanting to see it firsthand. 'I don't want all of it. You can

33

have this,' and threw a pair of red lace panties at him. 'These were in the glove box. They may not be Betty Jean's, but I can assure you, they aren't mine.'

"'You can't have everything!' Jim Bob yelled, spit slipping out the sides of his mouth.

"'You get the panties and your name. Everything else in or around the house is mine. I got it either through income from my paintings or as a gift from my father. He never did think much of you. I don't know if you ever noticed or not, but he's never so much as shared a cup of coffee with you, much less showed up at our wedding.'

"So the story goes that Jim Bob stomped the ceramic tile floor and shook his fists and 'But, but-ted' for about half an hour while Edna and her cousin waited for him to sign the divorce papers. It might have taken longer, but sweet Betty Jean showed up in short shorts and a crop top, already plump in the middle, bloated with child. Edna's cousin Travis Joe hissed 'statutory rape – she's a minor' and Jim Bob snatched the pen from Edna's hand. His fist was so tight that he actually tore the paper in two places when he signed his name.

"'I still don't see why you need the Caddie,' then handed

the papers to Travis Joe.

"There wasn't any shortage of witnesses for the last page of the divorce decree, or writ, or whatever it's called, either. There were so many, in fact, that they had to have several rounds of rock paper scissors to see who'd get the honor of witnessing."

Just then, the waitress popped in, taking advantage of Matthew catching his breath. "The usual for you two? And for the young man?"

"Root beers all around, right?" Matthew asked.

They all nodded and accepted the menus.

"So," Luke asked, "What happened next?"

"One week later, Edna had the pink Cadillac mounted to the biggest, stoutest sign pole in the state, maybe in the whole South. She had made arrangements to have the purchase of this sweet little café that Jim Bob was so fond of completed just minutes after the divorce papers were final. She told everyone who worked here at the time that if Jim Bob ever came in, they were to say, 'Sorry, sir, it looks like you'll have to eat your wife's cooking today,' and point at the 'We reserve the right to refuse service to anyone' sign posted right there in the foyer. See, it's still there." Matthew pointed to the black-framed notice, sitting to the right of the community bulletin board. She kept the name The Best Darned Diner, but we all call it The Pink Cadillac."

Luke chuckled. "So that's why and how…"

"Yup, and three and a half months later, Betty Jean's mama had her ninth granddaughter. Still to this day, no boys in that family. Unless they married into them."

5 Motorcycle Mama

"If you're sure you want to get right to work after eating such a big lunch… Golly, I've never seen anyone finish a whole plate of those biscuits and gravy," Maude said. "I'm sure your uncle would be more than happy to have you start Monday morning."

"Nah. I'm fine. Benji said Lewis would line me up at the big shop. I'm sure they'll let me know when it's time to quit. Sounds like Friday nights at your place are considered one of the perks for working here."

"True, we don't have much of a turnover. But I'm also pretty selective in the hiring process." Matthew chuckled. "Plus, lots of these guys have big extended families. Since my mechanics work a full forty-hour week and love having their weekends off for fishing and home projects, they don't take on any side work. They just tell their kin to get an appointment for repairs like everyone else. Since we fix it right the first time and give a 'family and friends' discount, we have as much work as we can handle. And then some. Once

37

again, I'm glad you made it here. Oh, and if you haven't already found a place to stay, the apartment above our garage is still available. It's just a little one room place with a toilet, sink, and shower, but should be big enough for you."

"Thanks. I think I'll take you up on that. I brought a sleeping bag just in case, but a real bed under me might feel nice for a change. No, I take that back. It *will* feel nice for a change!"

"You do remember where we live, don't you, dear?" Maude asked, her hand gentle on his shoulder.

"Is it still painted the prettiest buttercup yellow in town?"

"Yes and no. It's faded a bit, but still bright enough to show you the way home at midnight in the winter during a rainstorm. See you tonight. Don't work too hard. It's your first day and you don't need to be impressing me." Matt laughed. "You see, I'm taking the afternoon off and won't notice!"

Luke gave his aunt a hug, shook his uncle's hand, said, "See you tonight," and walked towards the 'big' shop.

Another fresh start. Luke looked up, whispered, 'Thank You, Lord,' and opened the door. His eyes closed as he inhaled the smells of diesel fuel and hydraulic oils, comforting odors that others might find repulsive. Suddenly, his hands twitched, eager to grab a wrench and tear something down.

"Hey, there," the Santa-looking man in coveralls said. "You must be Luke. I'm Lewis. From what I hear, all I need to do is hand you a work order, point out which tractor, and go back to whatever it is I have to do. Glad to have you on board."

Luke and Lewis shared a powerful but non-threatening handshake, then Lewis handed him coveralls and a work order. "Matthew said you could use his tools. His tool box is right there. He doesn't do much wrench pulling anymore and said you knew how to show tools the proper respect. Shop rags and absorbents are there, bathroom and clean up sinks are in the back, and if you have any questions, I shouldn't be too hard to find." Lewis patted his ample belly. "I'm glad I'm working in the Cat shop now. The dash panels on those little foreign cars were a bear to try to get into. Made me feel like I was working with baseball mitts on my hands."

***

It had been an easy yet satisfying job: unbolting all the outside decking and ladders from a used excavator. All the hoses were being swapped out, but before the new ones were installed, the tractor would be painted a gawd-awful pink. The new owner's entire fleet of trucks and tractors were the same color of Pepto Bismol pink and this recent purchase had to fit in. "I've never had one of my rigs stolen, and I can spot my jobsites from a mile up in the air," the owner said. "They may not be pretty to some, but my passion pink security system is efficient."

Just before four o'clock, Lewis came up to Luke, smiling. "Matthew said to give you a key. Just lock the door behind you when you leave. The key is in case you forgot something and have to let yourself back in. Oh, and you might want to bring a six pack of root beer when you come by tonight. There's usually plenty, but it makes Maude's eyes sparkle when she gets any kind of hostess gift."

***

Day was done now, and he was the only one left in the shop. Luke stretched the kinks out of his neck and shoulders. It had been a long time since he spent more than just a few minutes with a half-inch impact in his hand. He was used to diagnosing problems or going for test drives, letting others do the repairs.

Ten minutes of scrubbing with the pumice-laced cleanser and he was clean enough for family. He looked in the mirror and saw he had forgotten his face. The black bits of grime looked like enhanced freckles across his nose and cheeks. "Not good enough, even for family," he mumbled, then bent over the sink to scrub some more.

And then he heard it. It was horrid, like a symphony warming up with a set of leaky bag pipes thrown in. Someone was revving a motorcycle and it was seriously out of tune.

The noise was coming from the automotive shop. He still had his coveralls on. If it was Benji working on the bike, he was making it worse, not better. Hopefully, he wouldn't offend him by offering to help. Motorcycles were his passion and hearing one that was squalling like a cat in heat was intolerable.

It wasn't Benji seated on the stool next to the classic Indian Chief motorcycle, but Holly. "What are you doing here?" he asked, then realized that her back was to him.

He walked in front of her, then tapped on the handlebars, sending a slight tremor down the bike's frame, to get her attention. Her head snapped up, shocked that she wasn't alone. She had made sure the automotive shop was empty before bringing out her personal project, and the guys in the Cat shop always left for home without coming through the office.

"Beautiful," Luke said, as he looked down at the four-cylinder vee-engine. He caught her eye and repeated, "Beautiful. Is it yours?"

She nodded, her lips pursed in a frown, letting him know she wasn't happy about the intrusion.

"1940?" He moved back and looked at the rear suspension. "Oh, looks more like a '41 with that soft tail."

Holly couldn't help but smile. Not many people in the world, much less her little niche in North Carolina, knew as much about Indian motorcycles as she did. If Luke was as great a mechanic and diagnostician as Matt claimed, maybe he could figure out her timing problem. She stood up and held out her hand, figuratively offering her greatest treasure — and greatest frustration — to the dark-haired Adonis.

"Thanks. I'd like to see if I can help solve that misfiring problem, if you don't mind. These babies positively sing when they're in tune and are like a squalling baby when not." Luke quickly looked away to hide his blush. How embarrassing! She could read what he was saying. How could she know what a baby sounded like, happy or otherwise? And singing? If she had been born Deaf, she probably didn't even know what a song, good or bad, sounded like. Shoot!

Instead of dwelling on it, he bent over the carburetor, flipping the butterfly valve open and shut. It was sticky. Gummy fuel tarnish build-up. He could fix that. He stood up, pointed his finger at her and grinned. "I got this covered. I used to have the same problem with my Harley. The humidity here will play havoc with gas if you don't add a little fuel conditioner every other fill up or so."

Luke popped into the parts room, looked around and found it right away. "I'll just check the gas tank. Ah, good girl, you keep it topped off. You'll really run into problems if you let the crud that accumulates at the bottom of the tank get sucked up into the carb."

Holly watched Luke as he scurried to and from the parts room, reappearing with fuel conditioner. Dang. How stupid could she be? She hadn't used it in months. A sticky butterfly valve; that should have been the first thing she checked! She couldn't tell what he was saying to her; he probably knew she was Deaf by now, but had forgotten that he had to look at her for her to 'hear' him. But his attitude and smile let her know that he was trying to be helpful, not domineering or belittling. Cute and sweet, too. A rare combination in a young, good-looking male.

Luke poured some of the fuel treatment on the end of a grease rag and scrubbed the varnish build up from the valve, then poured the rest of it into the gas tank. He looked up and asked, "Ready?" then realized that he had been carrying on a conversation with her the whole time while looking away. Well, at least now she knew what he was doing.

Holly gave a quick nod to proceed, backing away so he could start the bike.

Varoom, varoom!

Holly put her hand on the exhaust pipe. Smooth. Nothing but purring vibration.

"Good idea," Luke said, looking deep into her eyes. "I tend to listen for problems in an engine, but feeling them is just as good, if not better. Are you a mechanic?"

Holly shrugged one shoulder, shook her head, then brought both shoulders up.

"Oh, well, if you don't know yet, but want to be one, you're in the right place to learn. However, with your office and advertising skills, I think Matthew would rather keep you down on the farm as a weekend shade tree mechanic."

Holly brought one hand up and covered her mouth in a silent giggle. She'd already been told that by both Matthew and Maude. She was cool with it, as long as she got to fix up her toys in a concrete-floored shop and not under the messy mulberry tree at her house.

"Do you mind if I take it for a spin?" Luke asked.

Holly pointed to the sissy seat on the back.

"Oh, I see that you upgraded to a motorcycle seat for two." When her answer was a blank look, Luke offered, "Or did it come that way?"

Holly smiled and nodded, then pointed to him and then the rear portion of the seat.

"Oh, so you want to drive and I ride on back?"

Her smirk of self-confidence was all it took for him to fall instantly in love. A motorcycle mama who wasn't afraid to take control. Shoot, he'd fall for her with that attitude even without that intriguing smile or the most gorgeous face and body he'd ever seen. Her beauty was definitely more than skin deep.

And she smelled good, too. Like leather and lilacs.

The most perfect woman ever.

6 The Perfect Friday

Heads turned as the two-person parade on one chain-driven vehicle breezed through town. The 1940's vintage Indian motorcycle, bright cherry red and complete with its original flared fender covers, would have been enough, but add that it was a gorgeous blonde in front, driving, and a raven-haired male who looked like he just popped off the cover of a romance paperback behind her, holding onto her shoulders... Well, folks everywhere were staring in amazement.

He was the new guy in town but couldn't be happier about the spectacle the two of them were creating, although he did feel bad about the old guy who fell off the curb as he left the barber shop because he was gawking at them. Luke started to tap her on the shoulder to ask, 'Where to next?' then realized she wouldn't be able to hear him, even if their helmets weren't in the way. Instead, he leaned forward just a little and relaxed into her.

Holly tensed momentarily when she felt Luke's warm

body come nearer. She wasn't looking for a lover, a boyfriend, or even a close friend. She had Benji as her confidant and 'Friday night videos at Maude and Matt's' buddy. Her tension eased when she realized he hadn't progressed beyond that initial body-to-body touching. No groping, stroking, or chest heaving that indicated he was sighing, wanting more from her. He was simply content. Content to have her in control.

Cool. She could get used to that. Nothing fast or flirty, but not sterile or innocent like a brother, either. An unexpected sigh slipped out. Oh, well. She'd let him make the next move.

Maybe.

***

Holly pulled up in front of the brightest yellow house in town, if not the whole state. She snapped off her chin strap, removed her red, white and blue helmet, then bowed flamboyantly, sweeping her right arm out, presenting the home of Matthew and Maude to their nephew, Luke.

"Why, thank you, my Lady Holly. It was most generous of you to share your ride with me." His face fell. "Shoot. I didn't bring anything to the party. Lewis mentioned something about root beer…"

Holly reached into her leather jacket and pulled out a fistful of straws. "Pixie sticks?" he asked.

She replied with a brief nod and an uninhibited smile, then separated the bundle, giving him half.

Matthew appeared at the screen door. "Here they are, Maude. I told you not to worry. Besides, old Kelso down at the barber shop called me and said he saw Holly riding down the street with a young buck seated behind her. Said he just about broke his neck coming out for a closer look. Come on in, you two. There's just the five of us tonight. I guess everyone else went to the Loews to see the latest Godzilla remake. The show's just about to start. I tried talking Maude into chili dogs for a change, but she says they're too messy to eat when watching a movie. So, it's corn dogs and mustard again." Matthew leaned in closer to the couple, looked Holly in the eye, and said, "Don't worry. I'll make it up to you at the barbecue. You did remember to bring something for Maude, right?"

Holly and Luke held out the straws filled with flavored sugar crystals. "Ah, my favorite dessert: dehydrated Jell-O.

At least, right now it's my favorite." He took three of the straws and shoved them in his shirt pocket. "Grab a bite to eat, and then it's showtime!"

Luke joined Benji in the kitchen while Maude picked through the straws Holly held out. "I like the grape ones best. I just have to remember to run in and brush my teeth right away after I'm done. Matthew loves to tease me about my purple tongue and teeth. That man..." She sighed deeply and turned to watch as her husband plopped down in his recliner covered with NASCAR blanket throws. "I hope he never grows up. I love him just the way he is."

"We already ate," Matt called out from the family room, "but there's corn dogs and mustard, pickles and popcorn there on the sideboard. Go ahead and fill up a plate. You can eat in here if you'd like."

Benji leaned close to Luke and whispered, "Ye'd better eat in here. Believe us both," he looked to Holly who had been watching the conversation; she nodded in agreement, "lots less messy."

Holly took a big, puffy piece of popcorn and sniffed it, then dropped it in the trash and shook her head at Benji.

"Scorched again," Benji said to Luke. "Eat at yer own

risk. Don't worry about wasting food, either. The squirrels love this place. I dinna ken if they eat leftover corn dogs or not because there's never been any, but they're verra happy with the popped corn, burnt or not."

The three of them wolfed down the casual dinner fare, washing the salty food down with canned root beer. 'She must have grown up with brothers,' Luke surmised, nodding at Holly, 'because she sure isn't bashful about eating in front of guys.'

Maude rearranged the pillows on her recliner before settling in. "Well, come on in and get comfortable." She pointed to the recliners she and Matthew were in. "Any other chairs in the house are fair game. Or you can grab a bunch of pillows and make a nest. That beanbag chair in the corner is big enough for two. Drag it in here if you'd like."

"This is fine for me," Benji said, and tossed three throw pillows in a heap next to the wall, then looked at Luke and winked.

Holly grabbed the oversized Team Al Unser logoed beanbag chair and dragged it to the middle of the room. She caught Benji's eye and held it.

Shoot! Had he been too obvious in setting them up? He

didn't mean to be offensive. Yes, they usually cuddled up in that chair together, but she was due—heck, past due—in the date department. At least with Luke and the Friday Night Videos at Matt and Maude's scenario, she'd be supervised. She was as safe as she could be.

Holly glared at him, clenched her teeth, and curled her lips into a silent growl, 'I know what you're up to,' she indicated, then transitioned into a coy smirk and a wink. 'Thanks, big little brother.'

"You'd better get into that beanbag contraption first, Luke, or you'll be bouncing Holly right out of it." Maude tossed one of the colorful NASCAR blanket throws to Benji, then one to Luke who was squatted next to the amorphous contraption, trying to figure a graceful way to get into — or was that onto? — it.

Benji said, "Just back up next to it, then sort of roll onto it. Once yer comfortable, Holly can get in. It's a two-step process, gettin' two people into one of those, but verra nice once yer situated. At least it is until one of ye moves."

Luke adjusted his position, making sure there was room for Holly, when he felt the blanket being tugged out of his hand. "Get in there, Holly," Maude said, "and I'll throw this over the both of you. Don't be afraid of him. He won't bite."

Luke closed his eyes as he felt his face redden. He knew Holly was probably embarrassed, too. He sneaked a peek at her and saw her eyes were shining with mirth. Holly looked back at him, opened her mouth and mimed a dog barking, then leaned sideways and pretended to bite his arm.

"Knock it off, you two," Matthew said brightly. "I've already fast forwarded past all those darned previews and now it's time to get Mars Attacks under way, tonight's feature movie for our Fabulous Friday Night Cinema."

It hadn't been in his plans, but Holly and Luke hitting it off couldn't have made him happier. He knew Luke was a good kid, and hopefully had all his wild oats sown. He and Maude didn't have an heir but leaving him in charge of the business would be perfect, especially with Holly running the back office. Now maybe he could talk his wife into buying a fancy Winnebago and making that road trip to the west coast by way of the Grand Canyon. Life's dreams aren't necessarily unobtainable. It's just that sometimes they take longer to achieve than we'd like.

"Make sure you put it on closed captioning, Matthew. You know I won't be able to hear the movie once you fall asleep and start snoring."

"I do not fall asleep during the movies. I may rest my eyes a bit…"

Maude's tsk-tsking caused Matthew to revise his remark. "Okay. Let's just say I don't fall asleep during a *good* movie. The man at the Wal-Mart said this one was going to be a classic. He saw it at the Loews a while back and just about peed himself laughing."

"Well, I guess that's as good a recommendation as we're gonna get. Go ahead and hit play." Maude rearranged her lap blanket, then kicked out her recliner. "I'm ready when you are."

It really was a good movie, but about half-way through, Luke started getting uncomfortable. Each belly laugh made the urge to pee stronger, but he didn't want to ruin the mood. Holly was snuggled up against him, their hands touching, pinkie to pinkie. If his intuition was right, she was letting him know she was available. He'd been on enough dates to be able to sense the vibes of a female who didn't want to be with him as well as those of one who just wanted to get her jollies then kick him to the curb. Holly was neither of these. It was as if the two of them were on the same biorhythm, breathing, sighing…

Click!

"Okay, enough is enough," Maude said. All eyes were on her as she stood up. "What? I'm not turning the movie off. I just need to use the ladies' room. And I'm sure I'm not the only one. Holly, go ahead and use the one down the hall. You men can go outside and use the hickory john."

"Wait. What?" Luke asked as he fell sideways off the bean bag chair, Holly's sudden departure to the bathroom having left him without support.

"The hickory tree. Get it?" Benji chided, offering him a hand up.

Matthew had already left and come back inside. "Next," he said to the two as he held open the back door.

"Now don't you be sitting down and getting comfortable just yet, Matthew. I have a little something set aside for first dessert. I think I'll have second dessert later, my grape Pixie sticks." Maude handed him a small serving tray with five orange sherbet and vanilla ice cream bars.

"Grab your dessert before you sit down, folks," Matt said. He set the tray on the table and took the wrapper off his bar. "Dinner on a stick, then dessert on a stick. What will they think of next?"

Everyone sat down, ice cream in hand, got comfortable with pillows, bean bag chair, or recliner, and Matthew restarted the movie. Luke had his treat gone in six bites, then slapped his head in pain. Brain freeze. He looked sideways to see if she had seen.

Holly knew what had happened and was smiling as she slid the ice cream-coated stick out of her mouth, swallowed, then opened up and put it back in.

The erotic nature of what she was doing had Luke's lower body responding. Is that why Maude had thrown a blanket over them? He quickly concentrated on the agony of brain freeze, then leaned back and groaned.

She knew she was driving him nuts with the way she was eating her popsicle. She wasn't doing it on purpose. Well, not really. It's how she always ate ice cream when it wasn't in a bowl. She licked all around a cone, too. Just the fact that he had thought to look over at her was flattery. He was gorgeous and surely knew it, but the great thing about Luke was he didn't act it. She sneaked another glance at him. Now he had his popsicle stick in his mouth, switching it from side to side, thrusting it with his tongue from one corner to the other. She squirmed unconsciously, then made herself relax and stay put. Now who was making who uncomfortable?

Slim Whitman yodeling Indian Love Call—the alien-slaying warbling as obnoxious over the speakers as it was supposed to be to the Martians—distracted both Luke and Holly from their unintended sexual arousals. Holly's belly laughs and giggles were silent, but just as muscle jiggling as Luke's. Yes, they were comfortable with each other.

At one point, Luke's back started to ache so much, he had to change positions.

As soon as she felt him move to sit up, Holly followed suit. She'd been aching for ten minutes, at least, but didn't want to lose that bare skin on bare skin contact, even if it was just arm-to-arm. She leaned forward to stretch out as Luke sat up straight, his arms reaching out side-to-side. When he slipped down to his original position, she decided it was time to take the lead. She turned sideways slightly and curled into his chest. Her view of the show was limited, but she didn't care.

Luke smoothed Holly's blonde hair away from his mouth, back onto her head. He'd rather lean down and kiss it out of the way, but he didn't want an audience when the time came. And by the way her hand had just reached across his belly and stuck a finger in his belt loop, it looked like she was game for a second round. He had been claimed.

***

"Well, I didn't pee my pants laughing, but that was a cute movie. I was thinking about rerunning a classic and making this a double feature night, but I decided I'd go to bed early so I could spend a little time in the shop tomorrow. The mayor said he wanted to take the missus for a ride upstate in the Malibu on Sunday. So, rather than have you work tomorrow, Benji, I decided to take a little hands-on break. You take some time off. I know you're always talkin' about goin' fishing, but I haven't seen you with a rod in your hand since you got here."

Benji's mouth twitched in embarrassment. "I never got around to buyin' one. I jest peel back the rough bark from a tough, straight limb, screw a couple eye bolts in, and run my line through them. I don't need to be catchin' more than I can eat, so this way I'm givin' the fish a fair chance of not getting' caught."

"On your way out, pick up my pole and tackle box there just inside the garage door. Do some real fishin'. And if you catch too many, well, I guess we'll just have to have a fish fry." Matthew laughed as the thought came to me. "I wonder if you could fix fish on a stick? It'd go well with the ice cream on a stick we had tonight."

"I dinna ken, but I do pretty fair with corn meal, salt, and fat back. Or cooking oil. Whatever ye have on hand, I'm sure will be fine. Thank ye for the great evening, and I'll see ye Monday. Any fish I catch I'll clean and keep in the freezer until yer ready fer me to cook 'em. Luke, I guess yer already home, or close enough to it. Holly, I'd ask if ye wanted me to drive ye home, but with the monster motorcycle of yers runnin' so smooth now, I feel as if I'd be insulting ye."

Holly saluted Benji, agreeing with his remarks, then walked over to Maude and gave her a big hug. "Where's mine?" Matthew asked, then backed away and extended his hand. She was his friend, but still his employee.

Luke looked around, his eyes cast down at the ground, avoided the others curious gazes about how he and Holly would say goodnight.

Holly clenched her jaws in frustration. Now she knew

how a goldfish felt. Well, she'd give them something to talk about. Or not. Suddenly, she felt ashamed. Surely everyone here wanted the best for her. They were hopeful, not judgmental.

Luke felt the tap on his shoulder and looked up. It was Holly, her mouth smiling, her eyes questioning.

"You know, for someone who doesn't talk much, you sure say a lot." He bent down and gave her a kiss on the forehead, then said to her without making a noise, "The next time I'll aim lower. And longer."

Holly answered him with a soft punch to the upper arm, then two thumbs up.

Yup. He wanted her.

7 Maude

Saturday

"I didn't like the idea of marrying Maude on her birthday," Matthew explained to Luke. "Hand me that 5/8" combo wrench, would you?"

Luke reached into the haphazard tool tray and spotted the light blue wrench. He had learned Matthew's color coding system early on. Having all sockets and wrenches 'numbered' with a color was much easier on the eyes than straining to see the etched-in numerals.

"And you were saying, about Aunt Maude's birthday..." Luke said, taking back the 9/16" wrench.

"Don't forget to wipe that puppy down good before you put it away... Anyhow, she was in a hurry to get married. The first Saturday that we'd both have free was two weeks away. To tell the truth, I was just as eager as she was. She liked to kiss almost as much—no, even more—than I did, but she wouldn't go all the way. 'You wouldn't respect me,' she said.

All the arguing in the world didn't work because, you know what? She was right. She said, 'How could you respect me if I didn't respect myself? I've always said I would save that special part of me for the man I'd be married to for the rest of my life.'"

Matthew rolled back under the rear end of the Malibu, used the combo wrench as a hammer, spat and sputtered as oily crud hit him in the face, then rolled back out. "Hand me that rag there, would you?"

Luke gave him his semi-clean grease rag. "So, you waited two weeks and then got married on her birthday?"

Matthew swiped the rag over his mustache, then stuck his tongue out and wiped a few wayward specks of road crud onto it. "Nope. I agreed with her line of reasoning. Didn't argue one bit. When I didn't, she said she was taking the next day off work and suggested I did, too. You see, we already had the marriage license. Got it the day after I proposed to her. She said it was so if I did ever change my mind, at least she'd have that piece of paper that said at least one man thought she was worthy of being a missus. Um, I think she was afraid she'd be an old maid like her sister. She was nothing like her sister, though…"

"You're rambling, Unc."

"No, I'm not. We took off to Black Mountain, got married right there in the magistrate's office. It wasn't until we were signing and dating the document that she realized it was her birthday. "Think how much money you'll save on gifts," she said "Plus, you're less likely to forget two big events if they're on the same day.'

"Yeah, right. That first year I forgot both of them. I think my back still hurts from sleeping on the couch for a week. I'll give her this, though. I never forgot the date again."

Matthew smiled and shook his head as he mused. "After we got married, we took off to the hills for our honeymoon. We got back to work two days later, bug bites all over. I mean it. Everywhere! She said she felt so ugly, all covered in calamine lotion, but she was the prettiest bride ever. Still is. And that was twenty years ago."

"Well, I can tell it's the truth. Not that you'd ever lie to me, but that glow you have when you talk about Maude never seems to fade. I can only hope I find someone as special." Luke groaned softly, embarrassed. He hadn't intended on getting into a mushy, romantic conversation: he was just wondering if there was going to be a barbecue this weekend or if he should make arrangements for a solo fishing trip.

"I'm sure there's a Miss Right out there for you. Might even be someone you already know." Matthew paused, cleared his throat for emphasis, then began again. "In the meantime, though, just treat every young woman as a lady. I'm sure the right one will appreciate it. Oh, and we're planning on the biggest barbecue you've ever seen tomorrow. I ordered a nice suckling pig from the butcher. I could use your help at the spit. Johnny's already dug the hole with that little backhoe of his, and we've been saving up hickory logs and trimmings for the fire. Gretchen is making the world's best German potato salad, and then there's the pie contest."

"What kind of pie contest?"

"Which one tastes the best, not a pie eating contest, you dolt. I thought you were past that stage of your life. Gluttony! Ugh!"

"I may have won the county pancake eating contests two years in a row, but now I'm careful about what I put in my body. So, it being your 20th anniversary and her birthday is why you're going overboard with the big barbecue?"

"Well, yes and no. She's worth all this and more. I kinda, sorta went overboard on buying goodies for her. I mean, they're for me, too. We enjoy watching movies on tape so much, I decided to buy her another VCR. I'll put the old one upstairs and the new one in the family room for our Friday night get togethers. And then there's the other gift. It's selfish of me, really, saying it's for her. She's needed a stove for a few months now. I went to Sears and ordered the fanciest one they had. You see, this way, I could get her the stove she's wanted and needed, and I could finally get a microwave. Stove and microwave combo. What will they think of next? She turned her nose up at getting a microwave for years, but I'm tired of the house smelling like scorched popcorn if I don't get the oil temperature just right when I make it on the stovetop. And that air popper she won at the church raffle makes popcorn that tastes so bland, I might as well be eating packing peanuts."

"Do you need help getting the new stove set up and the old one removed?"

"I sure do, Luke. I'd sure appreciate it if you'd give me a hand... and your strong back. I had the store to deliver it to Kelso's. It wouldn't be a surprise if I sent it to the house or even to the shop. Yup, after we finish with the mayor's ride, we can take the parts truck to Kelso's and pick up the new stove combo and VCR. It might be selfish of me, buying her a stove so she can make her fritters and the microwave so I can have perfect popcorn, but she insisted she could make that old range work for just a bit longer." Matthew started laughing out loud as realization hit him.

"I'll be gol darned. I just realized that she's been using that as an excuse to eat out for the last month!" He stuck his thumbs under his suspenders, then patted his tee shirt, stretched tight over his belly. "I'd better get her to cooking again or else I'm going to have to buy my clothes at Omar the Tentmaker. I already ran out of room on my belt, and button-up shirts gap too much. It's tee shirts and loose cut slacks for now, and basketball shorts as soon as I hit the house."

"Won't she be home when we bring it over?" Luke asked. "And what happened to all these wrenches? I put them back in order when I was done with them yesterday."

"Don't worry about Maude. She's out with some of her lady friends. Oh, and sorry 'bout the mess there. I dropped the tray when I was pulling it out of the toolbox. Dinged the dickens out of the edge of the tray, but it'll still fit in the box. I guess that's why they don't make tools out of glass. Hey, I think I found the problem. I'll pump some of that fancy new oil into the rear end and those gears will never know they've been apart. They'll be meshed like they've been broke in all over again."

"That's fine except for one thing," Luke said, dropping the other creeper to the ground. "It's me who'll be crawling under and filling that gear box. And do us both a favor. Never leave a disabled vehicle on the lift when you know you'll be working on the undersides of another car before that one's ready to come down. Two hoists and not one available. Geez, Unc."

"In my own defense, this one wasn't supposed to be ready for another week. But you're right. I should know better. I guess you won't be making the same mistake when you have your own place, will you?"

"Nope," Luke crowed, as he finished the fill job, torqueing the fill plug with his socket wrench. "I'll make new mistakes."

Matthew grinned. Great mechanic. Great attitude. Willingness to help others. Yup, he was the only contender for the new position of general manager. And the young man didn't have a greedy bone in his body.

***

"I guess I should have called Kelso before we came over, but he's always either here at the barber shop or upstairs there in his apartment. He said Sears made the delivery yesterday, so I thought we would be good to go."

Matthew knocked on the door again. It was unusual that the shop was closed on Saturdays, but maybe Kelso wasn't feeling well. "Maybe I should go upstairs and see if he's okay. He gave me a spare key a few years back, just in case something happened. Oh, Lord. I sure hope nothing happened…"

The door wasn't even locked, but one of the lobby chairs had been smashed to smithereens and a leg fragment used as a prop to keep the door closed. One good shoulder shove, and Luke had it opened.

Both men were speechless as they looked around the small two-chaired barber shop. Matthew kicked aside the broken glass and wooden chair remnants.

Matthew spoke softly, "It looks like someone got mad.

Real mad."

"But there's no blood," Luke said, hoping to make his uncle feel better. "Are you sure Kelso was supposed to be here?"

"I don't know why he wouldn't be. He's always open on Saturdays..."

Whoop, whoop.

The sound of the police siren letting off two short blasts got Luke and Matthew's attention.

"It's okay, officer. I know these two. They're friends," Kelso said, then quickly whispered to Matt, "This is your nephew, Luke, right?"

Matt nodded, then asked, "What happened here? And are you two all right?"

"Would you men wait outside while we look around," Officer Daily said. "This is a crime scene, plus it looks a bit hazardous. Do you have any security cameras on site, Kelso?"

"No, but it wouldn't do any good anyhow. I was in the bathroom in back at the time, but as soon as I saw those two punks come in with stockings over their heads, I was outta here. Sure glad I had an empty bladder, too, or I would have pissed my pants. I couldn't see their faces, but I could tell by the way they moved, they was youngsters. And strong, too. I peeked through the back window before I hightailed it to the station. I know that was dumb of me, but it was like I was hypnotized or something. I had to see what they was after. I guess having that door between them and me made me feel protected.

"Anyhow, they lifted that new stove of Matthew's like it was nothing. Then the one came back in and grabbed Maude's new VCR. Picked it up one-handed, carried it on his shoulder like it was a pack of toilet paper, then grabbed that chair with his other hand and used it to smash open my cash register. Not that he needed to smash anything. It pops right open when you hit the cash tendered key. Maybe he didn't know that, though. Like I said — young, strong, and dumb."

"Let's hope they're dumb enough to leave clues so they can get caught. What kind of car did you say they drove?" the other police officer asked.

"It was a big black Suburban. From the way they tossed that big stove in back, I'd say it only had the front seats in it. Smoked like a son-of-a-gun, too. Rattled and squeaked like it was held together with baling wire. They hit the brakes once, too. It was metal on metal, for sure. I tell you what. I wouldn't have to see that Suburban to recognize it: I'd know the sound of that rattletrap piece of garbage anywhere."

Matthew listened to Kelso's story with busy hands. If he wasn't wringing them, he was putting them in or taking them back out of his pockets, wiping one across his sweaty upper lip, finally clasping them together under his chin to keep them still.

One cop stepped inside to take pictures and look for fingerprints and clues while the older one continued to write in his notebook. "I'm sorry, Matthew, really I am," Kelso said "I don't know why they knew it was here. Shoot, it was a big secret. Only you, me, and Sears knew about those presents for Maude."

"Did I hear you right?" Office Daily asked, literally stepping into their conversation. "This was delivered by Sears?"

"I don't know if they're the ones who did the delivering. I mean, I saw the truck come in, but it didn't say Sears on it. I think they hire out the deliveries. But yes, it was purchased from Sears. Right, Matthew?"

Matthew nodded, still too shocked to speak. Luke put his

arm around his shoulder and gave him a hug. "Thanks, son," he said. "I needed that."

"There has been a rash of thefts lately, all the goods purchased from one of the larger retailers in the area, not just Sears. Then, right after delivery, always within a day, the products have been stolen."

Luke gulped as he realized he might have a major clue for the police. He stepped up to Office Daily. "I think I may have stumbled upon a stash of stolen goods, sir."

"What?" Matthew asked, his foggy stupor gone and replaced with a different kind of shock. "When? You just got here!"

Suddenly, Luke was the center of attention. The other officer had come over and was standing right behind him, just inches away, making a cop sandwich out of him. Shoot, one cop in front of him, poised with pen in hand, ready to give him the third degree, was stifling enough, but now there was this other one. The tension of having two police officers so close to him was overwhelming. Luke's brow was suddenly cold with sweat, his chest tight and getting worse by the second. He felt like he was suffocating. He wanted to say, 'Step back, you're in my personal space,' or 'Geez, dudes, quit crowding me,' but instead politely said, "Excuse me, sirs. I need to step out of the sun."

"Sorry about that, Luke," Officer Daily said. He recognized the signs of claustrophobia. He had it, too. His new partner was green and had a bit too much academy in him. Crowding a suspect so he didn't bolt was fine, but he'd heard about Luke for years. Matthew's nephew *could* have gone bad during his absence, but he didn't have that aura about him. Plus, he had decided to speak up rather than take the easy way out and stay mum. Yes, he seemed a decent sort.

"Bobby Ray, why don't you go in there and dust for prints on that cash register." The officer in charge turned back to Luke. "Feeling better now with a bit of fresh air?" Daily asked with a wink to Luke.

Luke realized the cop had seen what his problem was and had given him the break he needed. "Yes, sir. Thank you, sir. As I was saying, I think I know a good place to look for the stolen goods. Right after I came to town, I saw a suspicious young man escorting a young lady, rather a young woman, through a break in the chain link fence over at the old Carlisle place. I don't know if it's now a recycling center or it's still a metal hoarder's kingdom, but that's where they were headed. It turns out the young man didn't have the woman under duress, but she was *letting* him lead her to her own little haven. Trashy as it looked on the outside, she had an area set aside with stacks of boxes of VCRs, TVs, microwaves... I didn't get the chance to look up close, and they could have been empty boxes for all I know, but she was bragging about having her own little gang going, complete with cops on the take..."

Luke looked up to see the expression on Daily's face. There wasn't any. He finished writing in his steno notebook, then flipped it closed. "She sounds like a real winner, complete with an intimidation program. She probably threatened you, too."

"Well, yes, I guess she tried. When she threw that out about the cops on the take, I realized it was bullsh.. it was malarkey. Besides, I didn't have a car or motorcycle, so why would a cop pull me over? Nah, everything out of her mouth was a lie. I didn't even think about coming downtown and making a report or anything. I mean, it was just lots of boxes and a bleached-blonde bimbo with a foul mouth."

"Thanks for the heads up. I'll head over to the old

Carlisle place and see if there's anything visible from the outside that might show me a need to go inside. Right now, I don't have probable cause, but if you think of anything else, here's my card."

Luke looked at the card, then said, "Oh, she said her name is Tanya and that she's only been in town a couple of months. She's about yay high, brassy bleached blonde, and wears short shorts that must belong to her little sister. Other than that, there's nothing special about her."

Officer Daily had an 'ahh' moment as he realized who Luke was referring to. "I know who you're talking about. She's a floozy, all right. The guys down at the station have been talking about getting hit on by this tawdry little blonde." He rolled his eyes. "She even tried hitting on me! And I'm old enough to be her grandfather! Now that you've given me a head start on where all the goods are going, it shouldn't be too much trouble to flush her out."

Luke saluted the cop with the business card, then put it in his shirt pocket. "Matthew, I think we may be getting Maude's presents a few days late, but I'm pretty sure they haven't been sold yet. Let's finish that shopping list Maude gave you."

8 The Block Party

Sunday

"Looks almost as big as the feed at the county fair," Luke said. "Are you sure your neighbors aren't going to be mad about all the cars parked in front of their driveways?"

"Nope. I made sure to invite everyone in a twenty-house radius, more or less. See that long-haired buzzard over there? Old Man Johnson hasn't left his place in a year, at least. When I went up to his door and invited him, telling him we had a suckling pig roasting over hickory coals, he got all starry-eyed and giggly, looked like he'd just won the Publisher's Clearing House Sweepstakes. Now all we have to do is make sure Kelso doesn't get too close to him with his shears!"

Maude came up and started fussing with Matthew's shirt. "Matthew, dear, I know everyone knows who you are, but would you please wear this name tag? You need to set a good example. And I was thinking, we ought to have a big get together like this at least once a year, even if it isn't on my birthday/anniversary. Look over there. Even Edna and Betty Jean are talking to each other." Her eyes narrowed in suspicion. "Did you invite those two, because I know I sure didn't and they don't live in the neighborhood. The two ex-wives of Jim Bob Worthington; what were you thinking?"

Matthew started laughing so hard, he started coughing. "Now that that old whore-hound is out of town, I figured there wasn't a reason those two couldn't get along. Look at the way Edna's braiding Betty Jean's little girl's hair. Shoot, you'd think she was her aunt, at least."

"Well, I guess you're right. Life's too short to hold grudges. Asides, the two of them have lots to talk about, I'm sure. Here," Maude pressed Matthew's name tag onto his shirt, using the side of her fist like an iron, "Don't take it off, and if it comes off by itself, find me. I got lots more of them."

"Yes, ma'am. Now where'd that… Oh, there you are, Luke. I can save you some trouble. Holly's in the house, cutting up watermelon. Why don't you go in there and see if she needs a hand?"

"Am I that transparent, Unc?"

"Yes, and so is she. She made me promise to let you

know where she was."

"She said that? Really? With words?"

"With words? *Pfft!* You know Holly. She has absolutely the most expressive face. Heck, she could tell the whole story of the Wizard of Oz without making a sound, just using her body language."

"You got that right. I'll see you later. You know where I'll be."

"Right, wherever I see that white-blonde hair of hers, I'll know you'll be nearby. Now git!"

Matthew turned away and breathed a sigh of relief. "Dodged that bullet, didn't you, blabbermouth," he told himself. "She'd never forgive you."

***

Luke knew there were no lamps or batteries involved, but the ponytail on top of Holly's head shone like a beacon in the dark, calling to him. He remained in the doorway, watching as she sliced the melon a few times, then looked out the kitchen window, searching for someone.

Him.

He didn't want to startle her—she did have a big knife in

her hand, after all—but he did want to get her attention. *Click, click.* He flipped the light switch off and on twice.

She spun around, smiling from eyebrows to elbows, her shoulders hunched up to her neck in excitement.

All the indecision about how to approach her disappeared as instincts took over. He gathered her up like a puppy, snuggled his face under her bared neck, and sighed deeply, breathing in her lilacs and leather scent. He pulled back to look at her. "Do you wear perfume?" he asked, then felt foolish that he hadn't even said hello first.

Holly shook her head, then pointed to the bar of soap at the sink.

"Lilac-scented soap. I love it. I mean…"

The pair moved apart quickly as two little red-haired, freckle-faced girls came into the kitchen. "Where's the potty?" the older one asked.

"Just down the hall and to the right. You can't miss it; it's the room with a toilet in it," Luke said with a chuckle. "Now, where were we?"

Holly handed him her butcher knife and pointed to the other melon. She put up one finger, indicating she'd be right back, then grabbed the huge bowl of watermelon wedges.

Luke watched through the window as Holly wiggled and weaved her way through the crowd of smiling friends and neighbors. He never felt like he wanted to belong to a community—or even to one woman—before, but now he wanted both more than anything he'd ever lusted after in life, even motorcycles. How did his perception of what made a fantastic future change so quickly?

And then Holly turned around. She wasn't looking at him or even for him. She was reveling in the happiness of the crowd, her bright smile the reflection of the dozens around her. People of all ages crowded around her as she stooped to offer the watermelon first to the old woman in the wheelchair decorated with helium-filled balloons, then the younger children who had gathered around the miniature float. After the under four-foot-high crowd had finished getting theirs, Matthew came over and took the bowl from her. He looked toward the kitchen window, caught Luke's attention, and winked. "I'll need a fill up pretty quick, so get choppin'!" he hollered to him.

Luke replied by holding up the knife with one hand, beckoning Holly with the other.

"Sure, call the woman in to do the heavy work," Matthew

chided, but Holly wouldn't have cared, even if she knew what he had said. She wanted to be next to Luke, today and every day. Somehow, she was missing the man she had just met, as if they'd been separated for years. A chill ran up her arms. She turned back and looked at the crowd. 'Like a walrus in a sea of seals, you'll find your mate,' her crazy old grandmother used to tell her. Well, Luke didn't look like a walrus, but he sure stood out over all the other men she'd ever met, SEALS or otherwise.

Six men hoisted the pig off the spit apparatus and onto the meat cutting table. "It'll still be a while, folks. There's a lot of meat we have to get off this pig. Why don't some of you dig into that bag of Frisbees and footballs. If nothing else, you can throw them into the woods, then have the kids chase them down to get rid of some of that excess energy."

It was finally time to eat. Even though everyone was ravenous—the watermelon and chips had metabolized long ago—everyone, young and old, were courteous to each other. Matthew made a point of letting everyone over 60 fill his plate first, followed by parents with small children. Most of the adults let the teenagers and children go before them through the line of roasted corn, three kinds of potato salad, baked beans and more chips. I was obvious that there was plenty for all.

"Matthew looked over to Maude. "I could have sworn I bought enough for two big barbecues, but you were right. Today wasn't the day to go skimping on victuals. Once again, I'm sorry I don't have your presents. They were real nice ones, too. I'd show you the police report about how they were stolen, but then you'd find out what they were. I'm still hoping I can get them to you the next few days, though."

"You know I don't care about material 'stuff,' dear. This big party is more than enough for me. Shoot, more than enough for both of us." She reached out and snatched a fistful of air. "The love is so thick here today, you can just about grab a handful of it."

"Excuse me, sir. May I have a word with you?"

"Officer Daily! Welcome, welcome. We're not making too much noise, are we, sir?"

"No, no. At least, we haven't had any complaints. Then again, who's to complain? It looks like the whole neighborhood is here. It's just that I have something I'd like to talk with you about, in private if you don't mind," Daily said, then tipped his head to a spot devoid of partiers. "You, too,

Luke."

Luke grasped Holly's hand and gave it a tight squeeze, then followed the other two men. "Any luck?" he asked.

Daily nodded. "That little bit of info that Kelso thought was worthless really panned out. Seems that old Suburban had a transmission leak. It puddled there in front of the barber shop. We had probable cause that it was used in the theft, so followed the oily red trail to where you said Tanya's stash was. I don't want to interrupt your," Daily looked around at the multitude of people, "mega-banquet, but when you get done, would you come down to the station? I have some more paperwork to do on this, and then you can come with me and identify your goods. If you bring a truck or van, we should be able to load you up, then your wife can have her birthday presents before sundown."

Matthew breathed a big sigh of relief. "You don't know how much that means to me, Daily."

The officer chuckled. "Yes, I think I do. I'm married, too."

"Excuse me, sir," Luke said. "Were, um, any arrests made?"

"There were three. Seems the two young men involved in the theft still had their stocking masks stuffed in their back pockets. When I questioned them about why they were carrying nylons and mentioned that two men matching their descriptions had been seen robbing Kelso's Barber Shop, the one idiot said, 'But how could you tell it was us if we was wearing the masks?'"

"Really?" Matthew laughed. "He was that dumb?"

"Yes, he was. And the other was just as dumb or dumber. He pointed to Tanya and said she made them do it. It wasn't their idea, and that she was the one driving the car."

"Oh, boy," Luke said and blew out a big breath. "A confession before their Miranda Rights…"

"Bobby Ray was right on top of it, though. Pulled out his little card and read them all their rights pronto. Tanya was a little reluctant to agree that she had heard him until Bobby Ray got right in her face, just inches from her nose, and read them again. 'I'll keep repeating them, over and over again, until you tell me you understand. Now, do you understand, young lady?'

"'Yes, I do. I understand my rights. Now go get a breath mint, you, you…' And then she thought better of it. Didn't say another word except to tell those two idiots that if they said anything else, she'd have them castrated. Of course, then they both asked what that meant. So, all three of them are down at the county jail. I don't know how long it will be before bail is set, but because it's Sunday, I'm pretty sure they'll at least be spending the night down there."

"Let me go make excuses for us, and then we'll be right behind you, right, Luke?"

"Yes, sir. I'll tell Holly what's going on and have her save me a plate."

"No, no," Daily said. "Go ahead and eat first; they aren't going anywhere and neither are your gifts."

Matthew looked at Luke and tipped his head toward the buffet table. Luke shook his head. "No, I think the both of us will be right behind you. I don't think the food would set right until we have this case closed. Or at least, had the curtains pulled on it."

***

Maude pursed her lips and sighed. Part of her wanted to argue with him, saying he should delay the trip downtown, but she knew it was futile. "I'll set aside plates for both of you. The way those kids are going through that food, we may not have any leftovers."

Matthew kissed the top of her head, then lifted her chin to give her a slow, appreciative kiss. "I don't know what I did to deserve you, but I thank the Lord daily that you're in my life. Don't worry about us. Luke and I should be back before the pie contest. If not, save me some of Lucy's cherry pie."

"Don't worry about that. She brought one over just for you. I hid it in the back of the refrigerator. I marked the box 'liver and onions' to make sure no one got into it."

"And that's another reason I love you so much. You're beautiful *and* smart."

"Oh, you," Maude said and patted him on the upper arm. "Now git! Skedaddle out of her so you can hurry up and get back."

Luke came up to the two of them. "Kelso gave me the keys to his truck when I told him what was going on. He said there's no way you're getting out of your driveway; go ahead and take Old Blue. He said he had parked it down the road a bit so it didn't get dinged up, so he's pretty sure it isn't blocked in."

***

"Is this one of the rigs you fixed up?" Luke asked as he

ran his hand across the dash of the 1954 Ford F100. Matthew replied with a nod. "So, does it have the Y-block engine, too?"

"You'd better believe it does. I'm surprised he brought it to the party, much less is letting me drive it."

"Hmph. He knows that if you mess it up, you'll fix it for free. Anyhow, I'm sure the stove and VCR are still wrapped in cardboard and Styrofoam, so there won't be any dings or dents in the bed or the back of the cab. And, we're here already."

Officer Daily met the two in the parking lot. "Bobby Ray's already finished the paperwork. I'll lead the way to the site and you can follow."

In just minutes, the three men arrived. Stepping over the yellow police tape and into Tanya's hideout, they quickly located Matthew's goods.

"Well, lookie here. They didn't even pull off the shipping label. 'Matthew Morgan, care of Kelso's Barber Shop.' Oh, and here's that VCR. Looks like someone tried to scratch off your name, but didn't quite get the job done. Let me give you a hand there loading the stove into the back of that gorgeous truck, and then you can get back to your party."

"You're more than welcome to join us for some good eats when your shift is over," Matthew said. "We have a pie judging contest coming up pretty soon. Except there's no judging. We just load our plates and tell the bakers how great their pies are."

"No thanks. Besides, I was off shift before I got to your place. I wanted to see this case buttoned up, or nearly so, before I left on vacation. You see, I'm taking the wife on a second honeymoon up the coast. It's a bit early to watch leaves changing colors, but we'll have each other and no calls from work. What more could anyone ask?"

"Well, good health to the both of you and may the weather fairies deliver clear skies and pleasant breezes. And no hurricanes!"

The three men shook hands and parted company, the arrest of the thieves and return of the stolen presents put to rest in record time.

And with Tanya out of the picture, Luke didn't have to watch his back.

9 Heads Up

"Luke, can I talk to you a minute?"

Luke's head spun around, looking for the hoarse whisperer. The voice sounded familiar, and the person evidently knew him by name, but he couldn't place who he was.

"It's me, Robbie. Except you probably don't know me by name. I don't think we ever got around to proper introductions."

Luke bit back his shock. Robbie was the chunky young man he had met when he first hit town, the hapless fellow who he mistakenly chastised—actually punched — and did property damage to by breaking his switchblade. Could it have only been two weeks ago?

Robbie came out of the shadows, his head bowed down, but from what Luke could see of him, he didn't look too good.

"Are you okay? Who did this to you?" Luke asked, the hairs rising on the back of his neck in anger as he lifted the young man's chin and saw the damage.

"I'll be all right. I just got a little mouthy. Again. Tanya's muscle decided I needed a lesson in manners. Shoot, I think she just wanted to see me get hit. But that's not why I'm here. I know you know what kind of person she is. I mean, I watched you leave after our first, ahem, meeting. Shoot! I wish I had seen through her as quick as you did!"

Luke nodded in agreement, then frowned, urging him to continue.

"She's been especially ornery since she got out on bail. Always blabberin' about how she's gonna make you pay. Or you'll be sorry you ever crossed her. I don't know what you did, but it doesn't make any difference. Once she thinks you've done something she don't like..." Robbie shook his head, but didn't finish his thought. "Anyhow, I'm here about that kid who works in the garage with you, that tall red-headed kid."

"Benji?"

"Yeah, that's his name. I think he's in trouble. One of Tanya's goons knocked him over the head with a tire iron and dragged him into the back of her new old heap of trash. It looks like her old ride, but in even worse shape."

"When? Where'd they'd take him? Did they hurt him?

Was he bleeding? Well, spit it out!"

Luke realized that he wasn't giving Robbie a chance to speak. "Sorry, go on…"

"I don't think he was hurt too bad. I didn't see any blood, but, but…" Robbie started rubbing his forehead, pressing it hard as he searched for the words.

"What do you mean 'but, but'?"

"She had Cletus with her. He's new in town. Kinda dense and real mean, too. I think he's some sort of rodeo star or champion or whatever they call themselves. And he's always wearing pants so tight that…that you can tell what religion he is, and he's always showing off that big brass or silver or whatever it is, shiny belt buckle…"

Luke couldn't take the babbling any more. He put a hand on each side of Robbie's face. "Focus, dude. What did he win his buckle in?"

"He's a bullwhip champion. He was showing off to a bunch of kids in the park when Tanya saw him. She went over and talked to him for a while, whispered in his ear, got him all worked up. You know her…"

Robbie blushed at what he was about to say, then stopped and just pointed to his crotch. "She's nasty like that.

Promising what she won't deliver."

"But Benji! Do you have any idea where they took him?"

"I'm pretty sure they took him to that park just outside of town where she met Cletus. It's where they set up the trinkets he likes to take out with his whip. You know, knocking grapes off the bunch, snapping the head of a Barbie doll. Stupid stuff like that. The park's been shut down for repairs this week, so it's deserted. Just the way she likes it."

"Well, what are you waiting for? I can understand if you don't want to join me, but would you at least give me a lift?"

"No problem. And you're right. I don't ever want to have anything to do with her or any of her 'friends' again. I promised my mother I'd clean up my act, get my G.E.D., and then take a couple years at the community college. I hear they're recruiting for cop trainees. Hey, I may have made some dumb mistakes in my life, but I never got caught. Besides, I know what to look out for now."

10 Hidden Talents

Tanya looked over at Benji, tied to the tree, his back bright red and black from the welts and drying blood from his flogging. Cletus was at the cooler, drinking another cold beer. He had been whipping him so long, he had asked for a break. He complained that not only was he thirsty, but his neck and shoulder were cramping up. She knew, though, that he was holding back; he was working up to his A game. No one had ever come out of one of his thrashings without crying, or at least begging him to quit.

"Shit! Tanya, were you keeping count? I lost track. I can't remember if it was fifty or sixty. Damn. The way my shoulder feels, it's more like a hundred and fifty." He pulled his watch out of his pocket and looked down. "Naw. It's only fifty or sixty because it's not time for Monday Night Football yet. I'm going to call it at fifty because he hasn't squealed or pissed his pants yet."

"It's sixty-five, ye idiot!" Benji mumbled through his gag, then rested his forehead on the tree, doing his best not to faint.

"Hang in there, Benj," Luke called out, as he moved aside the brush to make a grand entrance. "We'll have you home, cleaned up and bandaged up in no time. We just have to take out the garbage first."

"You and what army?" Tanya asked. "And how'd you get in here?"

Luke felt a firm hand on his shoulder, then the sudden pressure of a blade at his Adam's apple. Claude had returned from his potty break in the trees. "Sorry about that boss. Won't happen again."

Tanya snorted at Luke. "Hey, pretty boy. I guess I was wrong about you. I saw the two of you riding around town on that big red bike. Maybe you do like women. Or maybe it's your little girlfriend here who plays for both teams." She looked away from Luke. "Hi, cutie."

Luke's eyes widened in shock as he followed her gaze. Tanya wasn't just talking about Holly, she was looking at her! His newly declared girlfriend had followed him here, and now Tanya was zeroing in on her. The bitch had already started her revenge by flogging Benji. It looked like Holly was next in line in her vile plot to hurt those he cared about. Holly didn't realize it, but she was in big danger.

"Tie him up, Claude. He won't be going anywhere for a while."

Tanya took her time walking around the new attendee to her sadism show. Luke's little girlfriend was hot—sizzling, smoking, make your eyes tear hot! She usually wasn't turned on by anything with boobs, but this gal even smelled good. 'Hmph,' escaped her lips as she checked out her new rival's chest. The platinum blonde's right boob was slightly bigger than her left. They must be the real deal. Suddenly, she was getting warm and moist and really wanted to spend some quality time with the woman who had Luke's affections. She chuckled. It would be all the sweeter if she took her away from him. Time to take up the challenge.

"Maybe your little friend here would like a taste," Tanya said and winked at Holly. "Turn him around, Claude, so he can get a better look."

Luke, immobilized by the knife at his neck, pivoted in place as the big oaf made him look at the two women. He was afraid he'd see Tanya hurting Holly, but nope, that wasn't the case. No guns or knives threatened his girlfriend, but what he saw turned his stomach.

Holly had just winked at Tanya and was now moving her hips like her underwear had snuck up where it shouldn't be. Shit! She was enjoying Tanya's perusal. She was flirting with her!

"Ooh, like that is it? Would you like to try your hand at a little flailing? Go ahead, I'm sure Cletus doesn't mind sharing, do you?"

Cletus gawked as Tanya picked up the whip from the picnic table and handed it to Holly. The platinum blonde's shoulders shuddered in anticipation, hands clutched together under her chin, Holly's smile as radiant as a child who had just received a puppy for Christmas.

"Oh, that's right," Tanya remarked at the lack of vocal response. "You're the dummy."

Holly choked back rage, covering her reaction with a non-committal shrug of indifference. She knew that now that Luke was incapacitated, she was Benji's only help. Losing her cool wouldn't help either of them. She reached out and took the whip.

"No funny business or 'Mud' will have a new hole to breathe out of…for a minute or two. At least, until he chokes to death on his own blood."

One more silent rage-covering shrug, then Holly added a phony smile of excitement. She played ignorant about how to handle her new 'toy,' and clutched it with two hands. She buggered up her first attempt, using an overhead approach, then smiled innocently. 'Help me,' her eyes asked.

Tanya called to Cletus. "Show her how it's done."

The big man set down his beer, then came over to Luke. "No funny business from you either. Did you tie Jerko's hands tight, Claude, and use square knots this time?"

The oaf corrected him. "Boss lady says his name's Mud. I thought it was Luke, but Mud seems to fit him better. Yeah, I tied him up real good with some of that clothesline rope from the hardware store. No way he can get out of those knots."

Luke held up his hands, showing the two of them how tight his bindings were, hiding the end he had worked loose in between his palms.

"Like this, Dummy," Cletus said, and cracked the whip, extinguishing one of the three citronella candles on the picnic table.

Holly nodded that she understood, flicked her wrist a couple times weakly—making sure to use the correct form—and then stood back.

She cracked the braided-leather weapon with finesse, snapping the metal-tipped fringed ends inches away from Benji's bare back, knowing that from their angle, the three tormentors couldn't see if it was making contact or not.

Benji flinched and screamed, not in pain, but in shock. He choked back the laugh of surprise and turned it into a shudder of fear. "That's enough!" he mumbled through his gag.

Tanya strolled over to her new love interest and smirked with satisfaction. "Oh, it looks as if we have an S & M mistress. Got much experience with whips, Dummy?"

Holly was glad that it had become second nature to cover her ire at the name 'dummy' with indifference. She had never 'heard' anyone call her that, but the words on those lips were worse than any swear words she had ever 'seen' with her eyes.

Holly grinned at the question, then twirled the whip handle back and forth, showing off her familiarity with it. This was becoming fun, toying with tricky Tanya.

"Okay. It looks like you know what you're doing. Let's see who's better. How about if you and Cletus play a game of tic-tac-toe on Benny's back?"

"It's Benji," Benji mumbled, then shook his head in self-admonishment at his conditioned response at being called the wrong name.

"Tic-tac-toe on Benji's back. You can be X's and Cletus can be O's. That's his favorite shape after all, isn't it, darling?"

Cletus gawked at his mistress's sudden show of affection, both her hands cupping her tank top-bound breasts, her mouth open and moving like a fish gasping for fresh water. Or a horny woman hungry for a big, hot salami. He'd waited for too long for her to put out. All her teasing and taunting—leaning over so he could see her breasts or intentionally rubbing up against the front of his pants—was finally over.

And, to make the mating even more enjoyable, they had an audience. No longer would he be a spectator to her kinky desires, watching those buff, bronze-bodied thieves try to please her with their wimpy man tools. He folded up his switchblade knife and stuffed it into his back pocket and used both hands to unbutton his pants.

"Shit!" 501 jeans looked hot and made a man's fly look as if he were hiding more of a package than it really was, but his short, lust-crazed fingers were losing the battle of the buttons. He ignored the thunk of a body hitting the ground, assuming that Claude had knocked out Luke to keep him under control.

"Whoa there, lover boy," Luke said, and grabbed one of Cletus's hands, slipping the clothesline noose over it. He had made use of the dazed whip snappers loss of focus and quickly bound both hands together, ending with a flourish. "Time!" he yelled and stuck both hands up in the air. Who said his calf-roping skills wouldn't come in handy in real life? "That had to be less than eight seconds!"

Luke looked over at Benji, still tied to the dusty old tamarisk tree. "Sorry. I kinda lost it. How are you doing there, bud?"

"I'll do better if someone will just give me a quickie divorce from this tree. Her bark is worse than her bite. Then again, she doesn't have any teeth…"

"What do you want me to do with her?" Holly asked. "It looks like the other one is out cold for a while."

Luke nearly dropped the knife he was using to cut Benji's bindings. He didn't know she could speak!

Her voice wasn't pitch perfect, and her words were loud

and clear, thick, but not *too* distinct or clear.

"I thought you were a dummy," Tanya said in disgust, her hands bound behind her back with Holly's dark blue paisley bandana.

Holly growled a low rumble worthy of a lioness guarding her prey from hyenas. She then stepped back, looked Tanya up and down, assessing her quickly. She paused, snorted silently, then issued a well-placed sideways kick to Tanya's midsection, knocking the wind out of her, and parking the slut's butt in the dirt where it belonged.

"What the..." Tanya gasped.

"Nope. I'm no dummy. There's a lot about me you don't know. And never will. You're going bye-bye for a long time. But don't worry. I hear they'll be giving you a whole new wardrobe. You'll be glad to hear that jumpsuits are back and you'll be wearing a new color. You see, orange is the new black and you'll be wearing it every day for the next ten to fifteen years. At least long enough that your hair will grow out to its true color. That is, unless they shave your head first. I hear there's been a real problem with lice down at the state pen for the last few months."

"Looks like you have everything under control here,"

100

Bobby Ray said as he entered the clearing with Daily's vacation replacement. "Almost," he added, as he stomped on Claude's back, keeping his face to the ground. "Charlie, give me a hand here and slap some bracelets on this one, then read him his rights. I'm really looking forward to taking this one back to the county jail."

He reached down and slid a zip tie around the hand Tanya had reached out, expecting a hand's up, then grabbed the other one and secured both hands before helping her to her feet. "You won't get off so quick this time, Missy. Oh, and just in case you forgot..."

Bobby Ray pulled out his card and reread her her Miranda Rights. "Do you understand?"

"Yeah, yeah," she said. "And you still need a breath mint."

"The ambulance is on the way, Bobby Ray. Do you want me to call for back up to haul these three in?"

"Nah, make them crowd together in the back seat. It'll be the last the boys will see of their little S&M boss mistress for a long time."

"I'll miss you, Tanya," Cletus called out.

"Shut up, idiot," she replied. "Can we get the hell out of

here?"

***

The next day

"Benji said not to worry about him. He's got a big pile of books he's been wanting to read. Maude had a great idea and set him up on an old fruit processing table. Covered it with chaise lounge mattresses so it was comfortable and narrowed it where his arms hung down so he had more mobility to turn pages. His face fits through the hole used for scraping pits and peelings into a bucket, so now he's set."

Holly caught Matthew's attention, then looked towards Luke and nodded knowingly.

"Yes, Holly, it's a good thing I have a replacement for Benji now that he's out of the picture for a few weeks. I don't want him coming back too soon. He's going to be marked, but with Maude doting over him, cleaning and dressing his wounds, at least he shouldn't have to worry about infections."

"But if I hadn't come to town, none of this would have happened..."

Holly punched him sharply in the upper arm and frowned.

Luke chuckled. "You're right. If I hadn't come to town, I

never would have met you."

Holly nodded and shook her finger at him.

"And you have a point there, too. Tanya and her goons would have found another victim, maybe one who didn't have friends who would come to the rescue."

"Yup. That's my nephew, Luke the unexpected."

"And my girlfriend, Holly the exceptional."

Epilogue

Spring 1999

He had never expected to find a Mrs. Wright, but she was definitely the one. One year and six months after they met, they were married. "Any woman who can put up with me for this long…

Holly tiptoed up and gave him a kiss on the cheek.

"And is still willing to kiss me, is definitely a keeper. You're right, Matthew, it does feel better calling her my wife, not just my girlfriend or even my fiancée."

"Now, I know you both love that bike of hers, and the little trailer you're towing behind it is cute and just the right size to carry your camping gear, but you need something more sensible. So, when you get back from your honeymoon tour of Route 66, I should have your new ride ready. Oh, and a '56 Nomad should be big enough for three or more. Maude says you're gonna need it pretty soon."

Holly's eyes widened in shock, then she frowned,

looking from Luke to Matthew, and back again.

"Nobody told us anything, Holly," Maude explained, "but you just did. Anyone who's known you for any time at all can see that you're glowing. And that 'who blabbed' look you just gave the men, well, I guess it's time to get out my crochet hooks and stash of yarn. Although I still may have to go to the yarn shop. I don't think I have the right kind for a baby blanket. Oh, think about it, Matthew: a baby at Christmas time."

Luke gathered Holly close, gave her a big squeeze, then bent her backwards in a romance-novel worthy smooch. He brought her back up and turned to the others. "And what a wonderful way to bring in the new year."

~~~The End~~~

THANK YOU!

Thanks for reading my story. If you'd like a chance at getting an ARC (advanced readers copy) of my upcoming books or find out random (and hopefully interesting) information, please sign up for **Time Travelers Anonymous**. I promise I won't plug up your inbox with loads of newsletters and I will not share your contact information with any other person or site.

http://bit.ly/dhNewsltr

MORE by Dani Haviland

If you'd like to find out more about the family in this story, there are lots of other books out there about them. Here they are in chronological order.

Naked in the Winter Wind: (rather lengthy novel) It all began with a tumble back in time to become involved with the fictional characters of a popular romance novel. A bottle of Fountain of Youth water, amnesia, abandonment, and adoptions complicated her new life in Revolutionary War era North Carolina.

Ha'Penny Jenny (historical novella) A bit more about the spunky young psychic, her new family from NITWW, and the rough life she endured before she met them.

Aye, I am a Fairy: (rather lengthy novel) James is not what Leah thinks he is, but the young British lord can help her in her time travel dilemma. Should she trust him?

Dances Naked: Directionally-challenged mature gentleman with a wry sense of humor is trying to get back to his family in the 21st century when he is found by a Cherokee hunting party. What will it take to get the chief to lead him to the Trees, the portal through time? Will his wit save him?

Little Bear and the Ladies (historical novella) The gentle 18th century trapper we first met in NITWW steps in to save the day for the survivors of a massacre. Now what's the bachelor supposed to do with so many women?

The Great Big Fairy: (lengthy novel) Benji finally returns to his grandparents in the 18th century, but he didn't plan on acquiring a very strong—and stubborn—female slave who can't—or won't—speak. The later adventures of Benji from **Pool Boy Wanted** and **Luke the Unexpected**.

Chasing Christmas (historical novella) A young Native American woman is rescued and brought into a new family where unexpected births, deaths and a marriage changes the dynamics of The Fairies Saga family.

Little Drummer Boy (historical novella) The young man wants to earn money as a scout but is told he's only good enough to be a drummer boy. Can Scout help the others find their way during one of the worst snowstorms of the 18th century?

Never Too Young (historical novella) Scout is older now, and has managed to earn enough to return to Jenny and provide her with a proper home, but will a con artist ruin his plans? And after the long separation, will she still be waiting for him?

Pool Boy Wanted: No Experience Preferred (a rather racy novella) He'd do anything to save his friend, and she knew it. Bad cougar! Find out about Benji's reference to bad experience with women from **Luke the Unexpected** here.

Time in a Little Blue Bottle (time travel 'mash up' novella) Elvis, Mark Twain, and the prime vampire are racing to get the bottle of Fountain of Youth water before sweet Bella and the youthful pickpocket. So why are time travelers Marty Melbourne and Master Simon interested?

Arlie Undercover – romantic suspense stories

A Stingray Christmas: (First book in the Arlie Undercover series) Anchorage detective on medical leave travels from Alaska to Arizona to see for the first time the son he'd fathered as an anonymous sperm donor. Great and rotten surprises await the cop with the smartest smartphone around.

The Biggest Heart Ever: (Book two in the Arlie Undercover series) When would Arlie learn that trying to do everything by himself could be deadly—and make Charlene a widow before they were married?

Always a Bigger Fish: (Book three in the Arlie Undercover series) Back in Alaska, Arlie finds out he's a target. Will vacationing detective Billy Burke (from THE FAIRIES SAGA) have information to help nab the scalper?

Stand-alone contemporary romances

Kit Kringle: An Alaskan Tale (Alaska novella) Kay moved to Alaska for the wrong reasons, then decided to stay and start her own business. What she hadn't planned on were prejudices and falling in love.

Be My Angel: (Oregon novella) Wyatt's dream to help save the wild mustangs began with the purchase of a rundown ranch in western Oregon. What he hadn't anticipated was being mesmerized by a sassy woman in a wheelchair.

Three Are One: (Alaska novella) The post chaplain tried to help the young widow adjust, but would his feelings for her and the search for his lost sister cause problems?

One Arctic Summer: (Alaska novella) The touch she never forgot. The summer of 1994 in Barrow, Alaska changed her forever. Could she ever go back? Would he still be there?

Dani Haviland has never been one to believe, "You can't do that!" She started her own business in 1994, selling tractor parts in Alaska, then segued to writing and publishing books, becoming a *USA Today* bestselling author in the process. She currently splits her time between Alaska and Oregon, tirelessly writing and gardening, publishing and promoting, while claiming to be 'retired.'

CONTACT INFO:

www.danihaviland.com

https://www.facebook.com/dani.haviland

Amazon Author page http://bit.ly/dhAuthor

Twitter @dani_haviland

Book Bub: http://bit.ly/BBDani

Goodreads http://bit.ly/2DHgdrds

Blog: http://bit.ly/DHbLog

Email: dani@danihaviland.com